Ka

Look for these
and other books about Karen
in the
Baby-sitters Little Sister series:

Little Sister

Karen's Toys
Ann M. Martin

Illustrations by Susan Tang

A
LITTLE APPLE
PAPERBACK

SCHOLASTIC INC.
New York Toronto London Auckland Sydney

ISBN 0-590-25998-9

12 11 10 9 8 7 6 5 4 3 2 1   5 6 7 8 9/9 0/0

Printed in the U.S.A.   40

First Scholastic printing, September 1995

The author gratefully acknowledges
Stephanie Calmenson
for her help
with this book.

Changes

"I am going outside to play! See you later," I called to my family as I ran out of my house.

It was a sunny September afternoon. I was at the little house. (I have two houses — a little house and a big house. I will tell you more about them later.)

When I got outside, I saw my friends. They were standing together looking down the block.

"What is going on?" I asked.

"The Jessups are moving away," replied Nancy Dawes.

Nancy is one of my two best friends. My other best friend is Hannie Papadakis. We call ourselves the Three Musketeers.

These are the rest of the kids who were outside: Bobby Gianelli, who used to be a bully, but is not so much of a bully anymore; Bobby's sister, Alicia, who is good friends with my little brother, Andrew (they are both four going on five); Kathryn Barnes, who is six; Kathryn's little brother, Willie, who is five.

Who am I? I am Karen Brewer. I am seven years old. I have blonde hair, blue eyes, and a bunch of freckles. Oh, yes. I wear glasses. I have two pairs. I wear my blue pair for reading. I wear my pink pair the rest of the time.

I took off my glasses and wiped them on my T-shirt. I could see everything better after that.

Just then, Andrew ran outside.

"Let's go say good-bye to our neighbors," I said.

I did not know the Jessups very well. But I was still sorry to see them go. I always feel sad when someone moves away.

We marched down the street to the Jessups' house. The movers had just closed up their truck. Mr. and Mrs. Jessup were walking to their car.

"Wait! Don't go yet," I called. "We came to say good-bye."

"That is so nice of you," said Mr. Jessup.

"Where are you going?" asked Andrew.

"We are moving to Florida," replied Mrs. Jessup. "It is warm there and we will be near our children and grandchildren."

"Good luck in your new house," said Nancy.

The Jessups thanked us and climbed into their car. As they started down the block, we waved and they waved back. Then they turned the corner and were gone.

"We forgot to ask them who is moving into their house," said Kathryn.

"Maybe some new kids will move in," said Bobby. "That would be cool."

We decided to walk around the neighborhood to see what else was going on.

Nothing much was happening on the next block. Or the block after that. Then we heard drilling and hammering. We raced ahead to see where the noise was coming from.

On the next block workers were moving heavy equipment onto a big construction site. They motioned for us to stay back.

"What are you building?" called Willie.

No one answered him. I do not think they could hear him over the noise. My friends and I decided to help him. On the count of three we shouted, *"What are you building?"*

The workers still could not hear us. They did not even look our way. Oh, well.

We headed back to our street. Things were getting exciting in the neighborhood. A lot of changes were going on. People moving out. Buildings going up. I could hardly wait to see what happened next.

Being a Two-Two

Remember when I told you I have two houses? Now I will tell you why.

A long time ago when I was really little I lived in one big house here in Stoney-brook, Connecticut, with Mommy, Daddy, and Andrew. Then Mommy and Daddy started fighting a lot. They explained to Andrew and me that they love us very much, but they could not get along with each other no matter how hard they tried. So they got a divorce.

Mommy moved with my brother and me to a little house not too far away. She met a nice man named Seth and they got married. That is how Seth became my stepfather.

After the divorce, Daddy stayed at the big house. (It is the house he grew up in.) He met someone nice, too. Her name is Elizabeth. She was married once before and has four children. She and Daddy got married. That is how Elizabeth became my stepmother.

Andrew and I switch houses every month — one month we live at the little house, the next month at the big house. We live at the little house with Mommy, Seth, Rocky (Seth's cat), Midgie (Seth's dog), Emily Junior (my pet rat), and Bob (Andrew's hermit crab).

We live at the big house with Daddy, Elizabeth, and Elizabeth's four children, who are my stepsister and stepbrothers. They are Kristy (she is thirteen and the best stepsister ever), David Michael (he is seven, like me), and Sam and Charlie (they are so old they are in high school).

I have another sister at the big house. Her name is Emily Michelle. She is two and a half. Emily was adopted from a far-away country called Vietnam. I love her a lot. That is why I named my pet rat after her.

The other person living at the big house is Nannie. She is Elizabeth's mother. She is a gigundoly wonderful stepgrandmother. She came to help take care of Emily. But really she helps take care of everyone.

Wait. I forgot to tell you about the pets at the big house. They are Shannon (David Michael's Bernese mountain dog puppy), Boo-Boo (Daddy's cranky cat), Crystal Light the Second (my goldfish), Goldfishie (Andrew's you-know-what), and Emily Junior and Bob (they go wherever Andrew and I go).

I have a special name for Andrew and me. I call us Andrew Two-Two and Karen

Two-Two. (I thought up those names after my teacher read a book to our class. It was called *Jacob Two-Two Meets the Hooded Fang*.) I gave us those names because we have two of so many things. We have two houses and two families, two mommies and two daddies, two cats and two dogs. We each have two sets of clothes and toys and books. I have two bicycles. Andrew has two tricycles. I have two stuffed cats. (Goosie lives at the little house. Moosie lives at the big house.) And you already know about my two best friends. Nancy lives next door to the little house. Hannie lives across the street and one house down from the big house. It is easier to switch houses when we have two sets of things because we do not have to carry so much back and forth.

Being a two-two works well for me most of the time. But little things can be a pain. For example, sometimes I want to see a movie when I am at one house. But everyone already saw it while I was at the other house.

A new movie was opening soon. Andrew and I really wanted to see it.

"Can we see *The Space Game* when it opens?" I asked.

"Is it supposed to be good?" asked Seth.

"The commercials on TV look exciting," I replied.

"We have not been to the movies in awhile. So let's all go together when it opens," said Mommy.

Andrew and I gave each other the thumbs-up sign. *Space Game*, here we come!

3

The Space Game

At breakfast on Wednesday, Mommy and Seth were each reading part of the newspaper. On the back of Seth's paper was a big advertisement. It said:

THE SPACE
GAME
The Action Starts This Friday
at a Theater Near You.

"Look! The movie we want to see is opening on Friday. Can we go to it?" I asked.

Mommy and Seth looked at each other and nodded.

"Yes, we can," said Mommy. "Friday is a good time to go because there is no school the next day."

"Karen, you have been to the movies a few times with Hannie and Nancy. So you can invite them to come as our guests if you would like," said Seth.

"Yippee! I will call them right now," I replied.

Hannie and Nancy were so excited. We made a plan to meet at my house on Friday at seven o'clock.

After school on Friday I got dressed up for my movie date. I wore new blue leggings, a white sweater, and a blue and white vest. Hannie and Nancy showed up right on time.

When we arrived at the theater, Seth bought tickets for Mommy, Andrew, and himself. Then he gave me money to pay for my friends and me so we could feel very grown-up.

"Three tickets to *The Space Game*, please," I said.

We found six seats together in the middle of the theater. First the previews came on. Two of the movies looked funny. One looked bor-ing!

Next some eerie music started playing. A green spaceship with purple and red rings sailed from the top of the screen down to the bottom. *The Space Game* was starting.

You know what? It was scary. The newspaper ad said to expect excitement, action, and adventure. But it forgot to say it was scary. Hannie, Nancy, and I were holding hands. Andrew was hanging on to Seth.

"Watch out! Look behind you!" we shouted.

The space creatures were called Tryops. They had three eyes each. One eye was in back of the heads. They had wheels instead of feet. They rolled backward or forward. The Tryops were heading toward some peo-

ple on a picnic. They were getting closer and closer. We did not know yet if the Tryops were friendly or mean.

Ooh, scary! I hid my head in Mommy's lap. Hannie and Nancy were covering their eyes. Then I saw them peeking through their fingers. I sat up and peeked with them.

"Girls, are you sure you want to stay?" whispered Mommy.

"Yes, we are sure," we whispered back.

The movie was scary. But it was fun! I was glad my friends had come along. If they had not, Mommy and Seth would probably have taken Andrew and me home.

Zap! Zap-zap! New space creatures called Gorgones had landed. They planned to take over Earth. They went after the Tryops with zappers.

Blam! Wham-blam! The Tryops shot back at them with ray-sprayers. They were trying to protect Earth from the Gorgones.

"Go, Tryops, go!" we cheered.

In the end, the Tryops chased the Gorgones away. The kids in the audience clapped and cheered as the friendly Tryops sailed home to their planet.

The lights came on and the credits rolled. I hummed along with the theme song. *La-dee-dah-dee! La-dee-dee!*

"Blam! Wham-blam!" said Andrew. He blasted an imaginary ray-sprayer as people left the theater.

"Andrew, please stop that," said Mommy. "That is not nice."

Andrew stopped his game.

"Who wants ice cream at the Rosebud Cafe?" asked Seth.

"Me!" we all replied.

Wow! A movie and ice cream, too. *La-dee-dah-hooray!*

Toys

"Tonight we are truly lovely ladies," I said to Hannie and Nancy.

Mommy and Seth let us have our own table at the Rosebud Cafe. We felt gigundoly grown-up. We each ordered an ice-cream sundae. But we asked for different flavors. I got Chocka-locka-Chocolate. Nancy got Banana-Dana-Twirl. Hannie got Cookie Crumbles 'n' Cream. Yum.

"I really liked that movie," said Hannie. "It was exciting."

"The Tryops were so cute," said Nancy.

"I wish they could move into the Jessups' house. Then we could play with them all the time," I said.

We talked and laughed and ate our ice cream. We were noisily scraping the bottoms of our dishes when Seth said it was time to go home. On the way to the car we passed the Unicorn Toy Store. It was closed, but we looked in the window.

"Wow, look at that!" I said. "The store is filled with *Space Game* toys."

There were games, T-shirts, mugs, and posters, too. Everything in the window was from the movie.

"I see a *real* ray-sprayer," said Andrew. *"Blam! Wham-blam!"*

"There is a zapper," said Hannie. "It looks just like the one in the movie."

"Can we buy some toys, Mommy? Can we, please?" I begged.

"I want a ray-sprayer! I want a ray-sprayer," said Andrew.

"I am sorry," said Mommy. "But these

18

toys are all weapons. We do not allow them in our house."

"But that zapper just blows bubbles," I said. I pointed to the tag that said "bubble-shooter."

"It still *looks* like a gun," replied Seth. "That is bad enough."

We could not buy toys then anyway. But maybe we could come back when the store was open. I had to find a way to convince Mommy and Seth to let Andrew and me buy a toy. Just one toy each. That was all.

"Can I buy something with my own money?" I asked.

"Only if it is not a weapon," said Mommy. "I do not even want to see a picture of a weapon."

I looked at the things in the window. Even the mugs and T-shirts had weapons on them.

I thought the no-gun rule was a very good one. But I wanted a *Space Game* toy badly. They looked like so much fun. And

I knew all my friends would have them. I decided to ask one more time.

"Can we break the rule just this once?" I said. "I know *real* guns are bad. But these are only toys. They will not hurt anyone."

"I am sorry," said Seth. "Your mother and I feel very strongly about this. We will not break our rule."

Boo and bullfrogs. I could tell it was time to go home.

Important News

By Wednesday, everyone in my neighborhood had seen *The Space Game*. And everyone had *Space Game* toys. Everyone except Andrew and me.

"*Blam! Wham-blam!*" said Bobby as he ran down the street. "Run for your life, you wicked Gorgone."

"*Zap! Zap-zap!*" said Nancy. Nancy's parents did not like guns, either. But even she was allowed to have a *Space Game* toy.

Andrew and I stood off to the side and

watched everyone playing. We felt very left out.

After awhile, Nancy said to me, "Do you want to try my zapper?"

"Thanks," I replied. "But I better not. If Mommy sees me with it, she will be angry."

Nancy went back to the game. The kids were all running around, shouting and laughing, aiming and firing. I thought about joining the game without a toy. But Andrew and I are not even allowed to point our fingers as guns.

I thought the kids would get tired of playing the game after awhile. But they did not. I got tired of watching, though.

"Um, Nancy, do you want to take a walk with me?" I asked.

"I am having fun playing," Nancy replied.

"But I cannot play with you. I am bored. You can bring your zapper. Maybe you will see an enemy space creature on the way," I said.

"Well, okay," replied Nancy. "I will go with you."

We walked past the Jessups' house. No one had moved in yet. We kept walking until we reached the construction site. Wide wooden panels were being put up around it. Soon the site would be hidden behind a wooden wall. We still did not know what was being built.

The site was pretty quiet and no dangerous machines were around. So we walked over to one of the workers. She was taking a coffee break.

"Could you tell us what you are building?" I asked.

"We are building some townhouses for people to live in," she replied. (She wore a nametag that said *Sally Riley*.)

"Why are you putting up a wall?" asked Nancy.

"It is a safety requirement," replied Sally. "Also a construction site can get pretty messy. We think a wall will be better for people in the neighborhood to look at."

"We are going to have a contest to make the wall look even nicer," said another worker. (His nametag said *Bill Grant*.)

"Really? What kind of contest will it be?" I asked. "Can we enter?"

"You sure can. We are going to put up signs about the contest tomorrow. But we can tell you about it now," said Sally.

She explained that anyone, or any group of people, could sign up for the contest. The panels would be assigned on a first come, first served basis.

"You will have three weeks to paint or decorate your panel," said Bill. "Then the panels will be judged and prizes will be handed out."

"That way the people in the neighborhood will have a beautiful wall to look at while we are working," said Sally.

Hmm. This contest sounded interesting. Maybe our friends would want to sign up. If we made our panel really beautiful, we could win a prize.

25

"Thanks for telling us about the contest," I said. "We have to go now. 'Bye!"

Nancy and I waved to Sally and Bill. Then we ran back to our block to tell our friends the important news.

Signing Up

"**H**ey, everyone!" I called. "Something exciting is going on at the construction site."

Nancy and I took turns telling our friends about the contest.

"Let's sign up for a panel," I said. "We can all work on it together."

Everyone wanted to join the contest. But no one wanted to think about it until we had signed up.

They were only interested in playing with their *Space Game* toys. I would be happy when we started working on the contest. Then Andrew and I would not be left out of the fun. I decided to sign us up the next day.

At home, I told Mommy about the contest.

"Will you help me sign up?" I asked.

"Of course," Mommy replied. "We can do it tomorrow after school."

When we reached the construction site the next day, Sally and Bill and a few other workers were hanging up fliers about the contest.

"Hi!" I said to Sally. "I am back to sign up for the contest. I am going to enter with my friends."

"That is terrific," said Sally. "The applications are in that trailer over there."

Mommy helped me fill out the application. We signed up for the ten years old and under age group. I told Mommy who was going to be in the group and she wrote down the names. We gave the application to a construction worker named Joe.

"Congratulations," he said. "You are the first one to sign up. We will give you panel number six. It is one of the ones in the center of the wall. That way everyone will be sure to see it."

"Thank you," I said.

When I got home, my friends were outside. They were playing with their *Space Game* toys again.

"We are signed up for the contest!" I announced. "We have to decide what to paint. Who wants to have a meeting?"

Everyone put down their weapons and gathered around. I told them that we had a center panel.

"So it has to be extra special," I said.

Alicia wanted to paint farm animals on the panel. Willie and Andrew wanted to paint cars and trucks.

"I know!" said Bobby. "We should paint a *Space Game* wall."

Oh, wow! In two seconds everyone agreed to that. We talked some more and decided to paint pictures of the Tryops and Gorgones.

"We will need lots of paints and brushes," said Nancy. "I think there is some paint in my basement."

"I know we have paints and brushes in our house," said Kathryn. "Our parents just painted the kitchen."

"We will need rags and buckets, too," I said.

It was Thursday. We decided to start painting on Monday after school. That gave us plenty of time to get the things we needed.

Big House Overnight

When I woke up Friday morning, Mommy came into my room to talk to me.

"Remember, you will be taking the schoolbus to the big house this afternoon," she said. "Seth and I are going to New York City overnight, and you will stay at Daddy's."

"Oh, boy. I almost forgot," I replied. "But I will not forget again."

Being a two-two, I did not have to pack anything. Everything I needed would already be at Daddy's.

It was fun to stay at the big house in the middle of a little-house month. I did not have to wait so long to see my big-house family. And something exciting was sure to be going on.

I was glad for another reason. I could probably find lots of paint and brushes at the big house. I was certain Daddy would let Andrew and me raid the garage.

On the bus to school, I told Nancy I would not be riding home with her.

Blam! Wham-blam! The kids were playing with their *Space Game* toys on the bus. They played all the way to school, then on the playground. When Hannie arrived, she joined the game with her zapper. Everyone was having fun running around. *Wham! Blam! Zap! Zap!*

I stood off to the side, watching. I was *not* having fun. While I was watching, I was thinking. I was thinking of a plan. It was a wonderful, sneaky plan. By the time I finished, I had one more reason to be happy I was going to the big house.

The day at school passed quickly. Before I knew it, I was on my way home.

"See you tomorrow," I said to Hannie when I reached the big house.

Nannie opened the door for me. She gave me a big hug. So did Daddy. (He works at home.) Then Emily ran to greet me.

"Hi, Emily. I am happy to see you!" I said.

Andrew was there, too. (Nannie had picked him up earlier from preschool.)

We had a snack of peanut butter on crackers, with apple juice. While we were eating, David Michael came home. A little while later, Kristy arrived. Then Sam and Charlie showed up. Finally Elizabeth came home. Everyone was happy to see Andrew and me. It felt like a party.

"Who would like pizza and salad for dinner?" asked Elizabeth.

Everyone did. We took votes on what kind of pizza to order. Broccoli and mushroom with extra cheese won.

Kristy and I helped make the salad. Then

I excused myself and ran upstairs. I needed to check on something.

I opened my big-house piggy bank. I counted the money inside. I had plenty for my plan.

Next, I talked to Daddy.

"Daddy, would you take Andrew and me to the toy store after dinner?" I asked. "It is open late and I would like to buy some things. I am going to spend my own money."

"I will be happy to take you," said Daddy.

"Thank you," I replied.

All right! My plan was working. So far, so good.

The Toy Store

"Hi, Mr. Mellon!" I said. Mr. Mellon is the owner of the Unicorn Toy Store.

"What brings you here today?" asked Mr. Mellon.

"I am going to buy *Space Game* toys for my brother and me," I replied.

"Oh, yes. Those toys are very popular," said Mr. Mellon.

I looked at Daddy. He did not say one word. That was good. It meant he did not know that the toys were against the rules at the little house.

Andrew gave me a funny look. I squeezed his hand to make sure he did not say anything.

We walked across the store to the *Space Game* display. Daddy stayed at the counter talking with Mr. Mellon.

"I do not understand," said Andrew. "How can you buy these toys for us? We are not allowed to have them."

"It will be okay as long as we leave them at the big house," I replied. "You just have to promise not to tell Mommy or Seth about them. The toys will be our secret."

Andrew did not look too happy about keeping a secret from Mommy and Seth. Then his eyes fell on the ray-sprayer. I knew he wanted it.

"Okay," he said. "I promise not to tell."

I checked out the toys and prices. I could buy one mini-ray-sprayer for Andrew and one mini-zapper for me.

I took them to the cash register and paid for them.

"Thank you for taking us to the store, Daddy," I said on the way out.

"You are welcome," Daddy replied. "Enjoy your new toys."

"Oh, we will."

We started to enjoy them as soon as we returned home.

Blam! Wham-blam!

Zap! Zap-zap!

We chased each other around the house. Then David Michael brought out *his* ray-sprayer.

"One for all, and all for the Gorgones!" I said. *Zap! Zap!*

"Tryops are tops!" cried David Michael. *Wham! Blam!*

"Time for bed, kids," said Daddy.

Wham. Blam. Zap. It was time to put our toys away.

I changed into my pajamas. Then I went to Andrew's room to say good night.

"That was fun, wasn't it?" I said.

"Really fun!" Andrew replied.

"Remember that the toys have to stay here. And we cannot mention them to Mommy and Seth," I said.

"I know," replied Andrew. "Good night, Karen."

"Sleep tight."

I felt bad about making Andrew keep a secret from Mommy and Seth. But he had had a very good time playing with his new ray-sprayer. I decided it was worth keeping one little secret.

I returned to my room and climbed into bed. Then I whispered in the dark, "Good night, Gorgones. Good night, Tryops. Sleep tight, wherever you are."

Caught!

After breakfast on Saturday, Andrew and I went to the front yard to play with our new *Space Game* toys. David Michael came outside, too. Then Hannie ran over.

Hannie and I both had Gorgone zappers. So we decided to make up a new ending to the movie. The Gorgones capture two Tryops and take them back to their planet to show them that they are really nice space creatures after all.

"Then the Tryops and the Gorgones

unite to fight injustices throughout the universe!" I said.

We made up an imaginary enemy.

"All red and yellow leaves on the lawn must be captured," said Hannie. "Let's go!"

Wham! Blam! Zap!

Hannie and I zapped those leaves with bubbles from our zappers. David Michael and Andrew sprayed them with water from their ray-sprayers. We were having a gigundoly fun morning!

Just then a car pulled into the driveway. Oh, no! It was Mommy. She was early. I had not expected her for at least another hour. I had been sure we would have time to put our new toys away before she arrived.

"Karen and Andrew, what *are* you doing?" asked Mommy when she stepped out of the car. "You know very well you are not allowed to play with toy guns. Where did you get them?"

Gulp. Maybe I could say we had found them in the backyard. Maybe I could say the Gorgones and Tryops gave them to us as presents. But I was already in trouble. Anyway, Daddy would tell her the truth.

"Well, you see, I had some money of my own saved up. So I bought the toys for Andrew and me. I did not think you would mind if we played with them here," I said.

"How did you get to the store?" asked Mommy.

"Daddy drove us," I replied.

"Would you please ask Daddy if he would come outside? I think we should talk about this together," said Mommy.

I did not want Mommy and Daddy to have a fight. Not because of me. I ran inside and found Daddy. I told him Mommy was upset. But I did not tell him why.

When Daddy came outside, Mommy explained the no-guns rule to him.

"I am sorry, Lisa. I did not know," said Daddy. He turned to me. "Karen, that was not right. I would never have let you buy these toys if they were against Mommy's rules. I do not like being put in the middle this way."

"I am sorry," I said. I really was, too. I had almost started a fight between Mommy and Daddy. That would have been awful.

"And Andrew, why didn't you say anything?" asked Mommy.

"Karen made me promise. And I wanted a toy," Andrew replied.

"Helping your little brother break the rules is not what a big sister is supposed to do," said Daddy.

"I am very angry with you, Karen," added Mommy. "We will decide on your punishment when we get home. Please go inside and get your things. I will wait for you in the car. But first, may I have those toys?"

"What are you going to do with them?" I asked. "You cannot just throw them away. They are brand-new toys."

"I am not sure what I will do with them

yet. All I know is that you and Andrew may not have them," said Mommy.

Andrew and I went inside to get our things and say good-bye to our big-house family. Then we slid into the car. I was in a very bad mood. Daddy stood on the front lawn and watched us drive away. I could see he was in a very bad mood, too.

Used Toys

After dinner, Mommy told me what my punishment would be.

"You will not be allowed to play with your friends after school for a week," she said.

One whole week? Usually this would be awful. But it was no fun playing with them anyway when they had *Space Game* toys and I did not. Then I remembered something important. The contest.

"Will I still be allowed to paint the panel with my friends?" I asked.

Mommy thought for a minute. Then she said, "Yes, you may. That is a worthwhile project to improve the neighborhood."

My conversation with Mommy was going pretty well. So I decided to ask another question.

"Did you decide what to do with our toys?"

Mommy had tossed the toys into the car when we were at the big house. They were still there.

"No. I have not decided," Mommy replied. "I will let you know when I do."

Then I got a gigundoly good idea.

"Can I sell them back to the store?" I asked.

"Mr. Mellon cannot take back used toys, Karen. Once a package is opened he cannot sell the toys to anyone else," Mommy said.

"Why not? The toys are practically new. We hardly used them."

"Would *you* want to play with a toy that had been opened?" asked Mommy.

"If there were no other toys left I would

not mind. Please let me try. Please," I begged.

"All right. I do not think it will work. But you can try," Mommy replied.

On Monday, Mommy drove Andrew and me to the toy store after school. Mommy and Andrew waited while I talked to Mr. Mellon.

"Hi, Mr. Mellon," I said. "I am back with the toys."

"Is something wrong with them?" he asked. He sounded worried.

"No. The toys are fine. But we are not allowed to have them. I would like to sell them back to you," I said.

"I am very sorry, Karen, but I cannot take back used toys. No one will buy a toy once the package has been opened."

Hmm. This sounded familiar. Mommy had said the very same thing.

"The toys work fine. It would be a shame to waste them," I said.

Mr. Mellon pointed to a sign over the cash register. It said, *"Returns must be accompanied by sales receipt. Only unopened or*

48

defective merchandise will be accepted.''

This was bad news. I did not have my receipt. My merchandise had been opened. And nothing was wrong with it.

"Could you put the toys back on the shelf? If you sell them, then you could give me my money back," I said.

"I am afraid I have to say no to you," said Mr. Mellon. "I cannot put opened toys on my shelf."

I was disappointed. But I remembered to be polite.

"Thank you, anyway," I said.

I left the store with the toys. When we got outside I handed them to Mommy.

"What are you going to do with them?" I asked.

"I am not sure. I will put them in the garage while I am deciding," replied Mommy. "And Karen, you and Andrew may not touch them."

"I promise I will not touch them, Mommy. I will not even look at them," I said.

Good Work

I kept my promise. I did not touch the toys. I did not look at them. I did not even think about them. I had other things on my mind.

It was Monday. It was the first day my friends and I could work on our panel. We met outside the little house at four o'clock with our supplies. We brought wagons to put everything in. There was no way we could carry all the paint, buckets, and brushes we had collected.

We pulled our wagons down the street

and headed for the construction site. When we arrived, some other kids were already at work. They were older kids, so we would not be competing with them.

The panel we were painting was in the center of the wall, where Joe had promised it would be. We knew it was our panel because our names were posted in the center. I was proud that my name was at the top of the list for everyone to see.

"This panel is a lot bigger than I thought it would be," said Bobby. "How are we going to reach the top?"

One of the older kids must have heard us because she called, "You can borrow our stepladder. We are finished using it for now."

"Thanks!" we replied.

We started out using colored chalk because it was easy to wipe off if we made a mistake. First we drew the outlines. Then we went to work drawing the faces.

"Have you heard what they are saying on TV and on the radio about *The Space*

Game?" asked Nancy. "They are saying some bad things. Some people think it is too violent."

"I heard that, too," said Bobby. "They do not think it is a good movie for kids to see. They say there are too many weapons in it."

"I liked it," said Alicia. "Tryops are funny."

"It is only make-believe," I pointed out. "Sometimes grown-ups worry too much."

And some grown-ups worry more than others, I thought. I wished Mommy and Seth were not such big worriers.

We talked a lot while we were working. We talked about our favorite parts of the movie, who we thought was going to move into the Jessups' house, and things that happened to us at school that day.

"When we are finished with our panel, we should take a picture of it," said Nancy.

"I will bring my picture to school for Show and Tell," said Willie.

We worked until the sun started going

PANEL # 6

KAREN BREWER
NANCY DAWES
ANDREW BREWER
BOBBY GIANELLI
ALICIA GIANELLI

down. Before we left, my friends and I stepped back to look at our panel. We had drawn two Tryops and two Gorgones on each side. We had done a good day's work.

"Somebody grab the end of this sheet," I called. "We need to cover our panel in case it rains."

We covered the panel with a plastic sheet. Then we walked home humming *The Space Game* theme song as loudly as we could.

New Neighbors

It was Saturday. We had worked on our panel all morning. It was looking better and better.

On the way home for lunch we passed the Jessups' house. It was not the Jessups' house anymore, though. A new family was moving in. I saw some kids. Five of them!

My friends and I stood around with our wagons, watching everyone run in and out of the house. The three youngest kids were girls. They looked about four, seven, and eight years old. The boys were about ten and twelve.

Finally the kids stopped running back and forth long enough to notice us. They stood and looked at us. We looked back at them. It was time for someone to say something. I decided that someone should be me.

"Hi," I said. "I am Karen Brewer. Who are you?"

The girl who looked about seven stepped forward and said, "I am Jackie Barton. These are my brothers and sisters."

"I am Lynda," said the older girl. "This is our sister, Meghan."

She pointed to her little sister. Meghan was holding a toy bear by the ear and swinging him back and forth. I did not think this was a very nice way to treat a bear even if he was a toy.

The boys were still just standing there.

"What are your names?" Bobby asked.

"I am Mark," said the older boy. "Do you

have older brothers and sisters?"

I told him I did, but they lived somewhere else.

"See you later, then," he said. He turned and went back to the house. His younger brother followed him.

"Wait. You did not tell us your name," said Andrew.

"My name is Eric," the boy called over his shoulder.

I guess Mark and Eric did not want to hang around with little kids like us.

"Do you live around here?" asked Lynda.

"We all live on this block," replied Kathryn.

"How come you have paint and stuff?"

We told the girls about the panel at the construction site.

"There is going to be a contest. The panels will be judged and the winners will get prizes," I said.

"Jackie, Lynda, Meghan!" called Mr. Barton. "We are going to town for lunch."

"Maybe we could play together later," said Nancy.

"Okay. We will see you when we get back," replied Jackie.

I was glad Nancy suggested playing together. I was not sure if I liked the Barton kids yet. But I wanted to find out.

After lunch, Nancy and I met Lynda and Jackie in front of their house. We played hopscotch. Their rules were different from ours. They would only play *their* way.

Then we jumped rope. Every time they missed, they said it was because we were turning the rope too fast.

Nancy and I were not having such a good time. So we said good-bye and went back to my house. We had a snack. Then we played in the yard. We were pretending to be Lovely Ladies when Lynda and Jackie showed up.

"Can we play with you?" asked Lynda.

"I guess," I replied.

We told them we were pretending to be

Lovely Ladies having tea in a fancy hotel.

"Won't you join us?" I said in my Lovely Lady voice.

We all sipped pretend tea and talked. Lynda and Jackie kept interrupting us. They were noisy. And bossy. They were not being Lovely Ladies at all.

But they were my new neighbors, so I tried my best to be friendly and nice. It was not easy.

13

An Invitation

It was almost dinnertime when I finally went inside the house. I washed up, then joined Mommy, Seth, and Andrew in the den. The six o'clock news was on TV. I walked in at just the right time.

"And now for a report on the hot new movie, *The Space Game*," said the newscaster. "The controversy is raging. Some parents are refusing to let their children see the movie because of its violence. The ratings board is considering changing the G rating to PG. What is your opinion? Call in your views to the phone number shown on your screen. Then tune in at eleven to hear what viewers like you have to say."

"Come, let's have dinner," said Mommy. "We will talk about the movie while we eat."

We turned off the TV, then sat down to meatballs and spaghetti with salad.

"*Two* meatballs, please," I said.

When everyone had been served, Seth said, "My opinion is that the rating for the movie should be changed. If I had known how violent *The Space Game* was, I would never have taken you kids to see it."

"I agree," said Mommy. "I want to know in advance what I am taking my children to see."

"But the movie was fun," I said. "I am glad we went."

"It could have been a lot less violent and *still* have been fun," replied Mommy.

"Weapons should not be seen as fun. They hurt and kill real people."

"A movie like that does not set a very good example. There are better ways to solve problems than shooting at one another. I think people should use words to solve problems instead of weapons. Don't you think so, kids?" asked Seth.

I stopped to think for a minute. Then I said, "You are right. If I used a gun every time I had a problem, I would not have any friends left!"

"You would not have a brother, either," said Andrew. (He thought this was a very funny joke.)

I was starting to understand why Mommy and Seth did not like *Space Game* toys. It did not seem like such a good idea to make believe you were hurting someone.

After dinner, I went outside to play with my friends while it was still light outside. (My week of punishment for buying the toys had ended the night before.) I did not mind anymore that I did not have a *Space Game* toy. I did not feel like shooting at my friends, even with a toy gun.

My friends were playing Outer Space Freeze Tag. I did not need a toy gun to play. Instead of shooting at my friends, I could tap them to make them freeze.

While we were playing, I noticed the Barton family getting out of their car. They had probably gone to town for dinner. I decided it was not easy moving to a new place. I made believe the Bartons were creatures from outer space landing on their new planet, Earth. It was my job to welcome them.

"Hey, everyone. I have an idea!" I said.

"What is it?" asked Kathryn.

"I think we should invite the Barton kids to work on the panel with us," I said. "We should be nice to them because they are new."

We took a vote. Everyone wanted to ask the Bartons to join us. We marched down the block and knocked on their door. Since it was my idea, I got to ask the question.

"Would you like to work on the panel and be in the contest with us?" I asked.

The Barton kids said yes. And you know what? They even said, "Thank you."

Action!

"Follow us!" I said to Jackie, Lynda, and Eric.

It was Sunday afternoon. We were taking three of the Barton kids to the construction site. (Meghan and Mark had decided not to come.) I could hardly wait to show them what we had done so far.

We led them to our panel and pulled down the plastic sheet.

"Ta-daa!" we said.

We had painted in most of the figures. But we had not started the background.

The Barton kids did not say one word. They just looked at our panel the way they had looked at us the day we met. Then Jackie shrugged her shoulders.

"It is boring," she said.

I could hardly believe my ears!

"How can Gorgones and Tryops be boring?" I asked.

"Nothing is happening," said Lynda. "The characters are just standing there."

"You need *action*. There was lots of action in the movie," said Eric.

"We better get to work," said Jackie. "Where are the paintbrushes?"

She did not even wait for us to answer her question. She marched straight to our wagon and took out a brush and a can of paint. She was being gigundoly bossy. Even *I* am not that bossy. (At least, I do not think I am.)

I was not so sure I wanted the Barton kids to help us after all. My friends looked worried, too.

But there was no stopping the Bartons.

Each was holding a brush dripping with paint. They aimed their brushes at the empty spaces on our panel. *Splat!* The spaces were not empty anymore.

We let the Barton kids work on one side of the panel, while we finished the characters on the other. Then we switched sides.

"We need another zapper over here," Eric said to Jackie.

"Use orange paint for that explosion. It should be really bright," said Lynda.

"Hey, watch out," said Bobby. "You are dripping paint on the Gorgone's head."

"You are dripping paint on *my* head," complained Alicia.

We hardly said another word to the Bartons while we painted. By the time we were ready to go home for supper, the background of our panel was filled with rockets shooting and weapons firing. Things were exploding all over the place.

I was not a happy painter.

15

A Brilliant Plan

My friends and I returned to the construction site after school on Monday. The Bartons came with us.

Bobby, Nancy, and I pulled off the plastic sheet. The panel did not even look like it was ours anymore.

"The new background is exciting," said Lynda. "But the rest still needs action."

The Bartons picked up their paintbrushes. They went to one side of the panel. We went to the other.

At first we did not notice what they were

doing. We were busy fixing up our characters.

"Psst. Take a look," whispered Nancy.

No. It could not be.

But it was.

The Bartons were changing our Gorgones and Tryops. They put weapons in their hands. They made the characters aim and fire at one another.

I was too angry to speak. So were my friends. We did not know what to do. First the Barton kids had said our painting was boring. Then they had changed it and made it violent. I was mad at the Barton kids. I decided it would be best to walk away. My friends followed me. We did not even say good-bye.

"What are we going to do?" asked Bobby.

"I do not know yet," I replied. "I am too angry to think."

I hurried down the block. I was so angry I felt as if steam were coming out of my ears. My friends had to run to keep up with me. Then all of a sudden I stopped short.

"I have an idea," I said. "We will wait until we see the Barton kids come home. Then we will go back to the panel and cover all the things we do not like with white paint. When it dries, we will put our picture back the way it was."

I thought this was one of my most brilliant plans ever. My friends agreed.

We decided to play in my backyard instead of in the front. That way the Barton kids would not see us when they returned home. We did not want them to come over. We took turns watching their house. Andrew's turn had just started when he saw them.

"They are back! They are back!" he said.

"Okay," I replied. "Let's go!"

We marched to the construction site. Our panel was covered with the plastic sheet. We pulled the cover off and got to work.

We painted over the things we did not like. As soon as the paint dried, we put our

picture back the way it had been. We stepped back to admire our work. We all agreed it was much better.

"We are finished here," I said. "Let's go home."

Something Good

A few days later, my little-house family was reading together in the den after dinner.

"Here is an article in today's paper about *The Space Game*," said Mommy.

"What does it say?" I asked.

"The writer agrees that the movie is too violent. She says that it has led to a lot of arguing. She wishes something good could come from all of this," Mommy said.

"Who is the writer?" asked Seth.

"Her name is Helen Goldman. She used

to be a teacher in the New York City public schools," Mommy replied. "I can tell that she cares a great deal about children."

The very next day, the newscaster on the six o'clock news said, "Stay tuned for the latest story on the hottest movie in town. We will be back after a word from our sponsors."

"A word? Try a few thousand words," said Seth.

He pushed a button on the remote switch to turn off the sound. Mommy and Seth do not like listening to commercials. When the news came back, Seth turned the sound up again.

"In response to a recent editorial in a local paper about violence in the movie *The Space Game*, concerned citizens in the area are getting involved," said the newscaster. "A toy gun drive is being organized now. A collection point has been set up at Stoneybrook's town hall where people can drop off toy guns. For each one collected, a local toy store will donate a brand-new nonviolent toy to a shelter in the nearby town of Stamford. So get out there and get involved. Drop off your toy guns this coming Saturday. Make *The Space Game* a fun game!"

"What a great idea!" I said. "It will be just like the toy drive at the family center."

I know about a center in New York City for people who do not have homes. Every year at Christmas, people donate new toys for Santa Claus to give as presents to the kids who live there.

"I want to give them my ray-sprayer," said Andrew.

"I will donate my zapper," I said. "I know we are not supposed to touch the toys, Mommy. But this is for a good cause. May we go to the garage and get them?"

"Of course you may," replied Mommy. "I am very happy that something good is coming from the movie after all."

The Toy Drive

On Saturday morning Andrew and I put our toys in the car, then drove with Mommy and Seth to town hall.

Lots of kids we knew were there. I saw kids from my big-house neighborhood and kids from my little-house neighborhood. I saw kids I knew from school, too. They were all in line waiting to drop their toys into the collection bin.

"Hi, Karen!" called Hannie. She and Nancy were in the middle of the line. They

moved back to where I was standing so we could wait together.

"This is such a good idea," said Nancy. "Someone said that almost a hundred toys have been collected so far."

"And there are still lots of people coming," I added.

When it was our turn, the Three Musketeers walked to the bin together. We counted to three, then said, "Good-bye, toy guns!"

We dropped our toys into the bin. Now three kids who might not have any toys at all were each going to get brand-new ones. That made me feel good.

"Look, there is a letter from the teacher who wrote to the newspaper," I said.

The letter was posted next to the collection bin. It said:

Dear Friends,

It was my wish that the arguing over the movie The Space Game *be turned into some-*

thing good. Your toy drive has made my wish come true. Thank you.

Sincerely,
Helen Goldman

"Now I am double-glad I gave away my zapper," I said. It is nice to make somebody's wish come true.

I could see Mommy waving to me from across the room.

"I have to go," I said to my friends.

"See you later," said Nancy.

" 'Bye," said Hannie.

On the way home, we heard on the radio that the toy drive committee expected over two hundred toy guns to be dropped off by noon when the collection ended. That meant that over two hundred new toys would be donated to the shelter. The drive was a big success.

A few minutes later we were driving along the street toward the construction site. I was glad no more pictures of rockets shooting or weapons firing were on our panel.

But as we got closer, I saw something strange. The panel was uncovered. The picture my friends and I had worked on was painted over. I saw pictures of rockets and weapons again. I had no trouble guessing who had put them there.

"That does it," I said to Andrew. "The painting war is on."

The Painting War

I did not say anything to Mommy or Seth about the painting war. This was between me and my friends, and the Barton kids. I rounded up my friends and told them what the Bartons had done.

"I cannot believe they did that!" cried Nancy.

"Who do they think they are?" said Kathryn.

"I say we paint the panel again right now," I said. "This is *war!*"

We marched to the construction site and

went to work. First we covered all the rockets and weapons with white paint. When that dried, we put our picture back again.

"That will show them," said Bobby. "They cannot paint over our picture and get away with it."

We checked our painting on Sunday morning. It was not the way we had left it. We had painted over *their* painting. Then they had painted over *ours*.

"No problem," I said. "We will just cover their painting and put ours back." (We were getting good at this.)

Guess which painting was on the panel on Monday. The Bartons'. We covered theirs and put ours back. They covered ours and put theirs back. Then ours was back. Then theirs was back.

Once we passed them in the street. They were splattered with paint. So were we. We did not say a word to each other.

On Thursday afternoon, we met at my house after school.

"The contest is Saturday afternoon," I

said. "It will be here before we know it."

"But our panel is in terrible shape," said Nancy.

It was true. We could hardly tell whose painting was there anymore. The panel was a muddy mess. The painting war was out of control.

"We have a problem on our hands," said Bobby.

"What are we going to do?" asked Andrew.

I remembered what Seth had said about solving problems. He had said words are better than weapons. My friends and I had not been using weapons to solve our problem with the Bartons. But we had not been using words, either. It was time to talk.

Working Together

First my friends and I talked to each other. I told them what Seth had said. I suggested we go to the Bartons' house so we could talk things over.

Everyone liked the idea. I was voted the spokesperson. Being a spokesperson is a very important job. But I was not worried. I knew I was up to it.

We decided what we wanted to say. Then we marched down the block and rang the Bartons' bell. Jackie answered it. Lynda and Eric were behind her.

"We were just on our way out," said Jackie. "We have someplace important to go."

We knew where they were going because they were wearing their painting clothes. I stepped forward and said what my friends and I had agreed I should say.

"We have a problem. We would like to talk about it. We hope you want to talk, too."

The Barton kids looked at each other and nodded.

"You are right," said Lynda. "We do have a problem. Talking is a good idea."

We sat down in the yard. The first thing we did was apologize to each other.

"We should not have covered up your painting just because we did not like it," I said.

"We should not have changed your painting in the first place. We should have talked to you about it," said Lynda.

We agreed that if we had used words instead of paintbrushes, we would not be

in the mess we were in now.

"The contest is on Saturday. There is no way we can win while our panel looks the way it does," said Eric.

"It is such a mess, we probably should not even *enter* the contest," said Kathryn.

"We can fix it if we work together," I said. "I know we can."

We agreed that if we were going to work together, we would have to compromise. My friends and I did not want any weapons on the panel. The Bartons did not want the panel to be boring. We tossed a lot of ideas around and came up with a stupendous plan. We decided to make a *Space Game* comic strip.

"We can make it really funny," I said. "Instead of weapons, the space creatures can throw pies at each other."

"They can squirt each other with water from hoses," said Lynda.

"This panel will not be one bit boring!" exclaimed Jackie.

"And it will not show any weapons,"

said Bobby. "You cannot get hurt with an apple pie."

"But you could get full if you ate one!" replied Andrew. (He thought this was another very funny joke.)

"Come on," said Eric. "We better get to work."

We hurried to the construction site. We had just enough time to paint the panel white before it started to get dark outside.

We returned on Friday after school, on Saturday morning, and again on Saturday after lunch. We worked together in one big group.

Making a comic strip is hard work. But we all agreed it was worth it. The judging was set for three o'clock that Saturday. At two-thirty, our panel was wet. But it was ready.

The Contest

We had just enough time to run home, change our clothes, and get back to the site for the judging.

A big crowd was already waiting when we arrived. My friends and I stood by our panel. We waved to our families, who were nearby. A man stepped onto a platform.

"Welcome, everyone," he said. "I am Jack Murphy, the construction site foreman. Behind me are the judges of today's contest."

He introduced our three construction site friends, Sally, Bill, and Joe.

"I would like to begin by thanking all of you who took part in this program," said Mr. Murphy. "When my workers and I leave your neighborhood, we hope you will be happy with the buildings we leave behind. In the meantime, things can get pretty messy. The beautiful panels you have contributed will be much nicer to look at over the next few months than our dirt, cement, and machines. And now it is time to begin."

Sally, Bill, and Joe walked from panel to panel. They took their time studying each one. On one panel were colorful flowers and trees. Another showed a line of children holding hands with a rainbow in the sky. Still another had a blue lake with sailboats on it.

When the judges reached our panel, they began to smile. Then they began to laugh. Our Gorgones and Tryops were funny. In the first scene they were waving their arms and arguing. Then they were throwing pies and spraying water at each other. In the last scene, they were shaking hands and clowning around.

There were several more panels for the judges to look at. By the time they returned to the platform, my friends and I were so nervous that we could hardly keep still.

It took a little while for the judges to make their decision. Finally, Mr. Murphy came back to announce the winners. There were three categories for each age group. He awarded prizes in the first and second categories. We did not win anything in either of those. I was beginning to wonder if we would win anything at all.

"And now for our third category," said Mr. Murphy. "In our under ten age group, the first place award for the Funniest Panel goes to number six, *The Gorgones and The Tryops.*"

Yippee! My friends and I jumped up and down so much that the judges could not even shake our hands. Sally hung the blue ribbon on our panel and waved to us instead. The ribbon looked gigundoly beautiful there.

I was happy our work would be on display for as long as the construction was going on.

When the judging was over, my friends and I walked home with our families.

"Seth and I are very proud of you," Mommy said to Andrew and me. "It could not have been easy for you and your friends to work on one panel together. But you found a way to work out your differences peacefully. Otherwise the panel could never have been as good as it is."

I knew we had not worked out our differences peacefully at first. But we had learned. That is the important thing.

When we reached our block we played a game of softball. Then Mr. and Mrs. Barton brought cookies outside for us. Mommy and Seth brought us lemonade. And all of us — old friends and new — had a party to celebrate winning first prize for the funniest panel in town.

About the Author

ANN M. MARTIN lives in New York City and loves animals, especially cats. She has two cats of her own, Mouse and Rosie.

Other books by Ann M. Martin that you might enjoy are *Stage Fright*; *Me and Katie (the Pest)*; and the books in *The Baby-sitters Club* series.

Ann likes ice cream and *I Love Lucy*. And she has her own little sister, whose name is Jane.

Little Sister

Don't miss #66

KAREN'S MONSTERS

"Um, Karen, what is that?" asked Hannie in a shaky voice.

I turned and saw . . . two red lights. They were blinking in the dining room. "Aughhh!" I screamed. "It is the monster! Frankenstone has come to life!"

The lights were moving toward us. Slowly, very slowly. I could see Frank's head. I could see his arm going up and down.

"Moooooahhhh-ha-ha!" groaned Frank.

"Eeeeee! Yikes!" shrieked Hannie and Nancy. They grabbed my hands.

"Charlie!" I called. "Charlie! Where are you? You made a better monster than you thought! He is *alive!*"

Nancy looked down the hallway. She knew where her room was. She walked toward it very slowly. Natalie ran by her. Omar ran by her. Ricky ran by her.

"Hey, slowpoke!" Ricky called to Nancy.

Nancy stopped outside Ms. Colman's room. She poked her head in the door.

"BOO!" shouted Bully Bobby.

"Aughh!" shrieked Nancy.

"Scared you, you baby," said Bobby. He glared at Nancy.

Nancy took another step into the room. She saw Natalie, Ricky, the Barkan twins, and some other kids she knew from kindergarten and first grade. And she saw a lot of kids she did not know.

"Good morning, boys and girls," said a grown-up's voice.

Standing in the doorway behind Nancy was Ms. Colman. She was smiling. She was smiling even though Ian Johnson was pretending to brush his hair with an eraser. And even though Audrey Green was giving herself a tattoo with a red Magic Maker. And even though Hank Reubens was tickling Leslie Morris and had made Leslie fall on the floor.

Nancy looked at Hannie. She was about to lean over and whisper, "Psst! Hey! Hannie Papadakis!"

But Hannie was busy whispering to Sara Ford who sat in front of her. Then Terri Barkan turned around and asked Hannie if she could borrow a pencil. And then Ricky passed a note to Hannie.

Nancy sighed. She gazed around the room. Who would be her second-grade best friend?

Little Sister™
by Ann M. Martin, author of *The Baby-sitters Club*®

More Titles... ➡

The Baby-sitters Little Sister titles continued...

❑	MQ44825-0	#29	Karen's Cartwheel	$2.75
❑	MQ45645-8	#30	Karen's Kittens	$2.75
❑	MQ45646-6	#31	Karen's Bully	$2.95
❑	MQ45647-4	#32	Karen's Pumpkin Patch	$2.95
❑	MQ45648-2	#33	Karen's Secret	$2.95
❑	MQ45650-4	#34	Karen's Snow Day	$2.95
❑	MQ45652-0	#35	Karen's Doll Hospital	$2.95
❑	MQ45651-2	#36	Karen's New Friend	$2.95
❑	MQ45653-9	#37	Karen's Tuba	$2.95
❑	MQ45655-5	#38	Karen's Big Lie	$2.95
❑	MQ45654-7	#39	Karen's Wedding	$2.95
❑	MQ47040-X	#40	Karen's Newspaper	$2.95
❑	MQ47041-8	#41	Karen's School	$2.95
❑	MQ47042-6	#42	Karen's Pizza Party	$2.95
❑	MQ46912-6	#43	Karen's Toothache	$2.95
❑	MQ47043-4	#44	Karen's Big Weekend	$2.95
❑	MQ47044-2	#45	Karen's Twin	$2.95
❑	MQ47045-0	#46	Karen's Baby-sitter	$2.95
❑	MQ43647-3		Karen's Wish Super Special #1	$2.95
❑	MQ44834-X		Karen's Plane Trip Super Special #2	$3.25
❑	MQ44827-7		Karen's Mystery Super Special #3	$2.95
❑	MQ45644-X		Karen's Three Musketeers Super Special #4	$2.95
❑	MQ45649-0		Karen's Baby Super Special #5	$3.25
❑	MQ46911-8		Karen's Campout Super Special #6	$3.25

Available wherever you buy books, or use this order form.

Welcome to
MS. COLMAN'S
Class

NANCY

BOBBY

KAREN

HANNIE

RICKY

Meet some new friends in a brand-new
series just right for <u>you</u>.
Starring **Baby-sitters Little Sister**
Karen Brewer...
and everyone else in the second grade.

Look for THE KIDS IN MS. COLMAN'S CLASS #1: TEACHERS PET.
Coming to your bookstore in September.

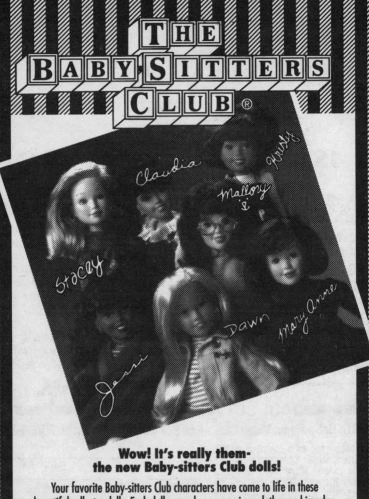